A Canvas Of Humanity

Samara

Ukiyoto Publishing

All global publishing rights are held by

Ukiyoto Publishing

Published in 2023

Content Copyright © Samara

ISBN 9789360498207

All rights reserved.
No part of this publication may be reproduced, transmitted, or stored in a retrieval system, in any form by any means, electronic, mechanical, photocopying, recording or otherwise, without the prior permission of the publisher.

The moral rights of the author have been asserted.

This is a work of fiction. Names, characters, businesses, places, events, locales, and incidents are either the products of the author's imagination or used in a fictitious manner. Any resemblance to actual persons, living or dead, or actual events is purely coincidental.

This book is sold subject to the condition that it shall not by way of trade or otherwise, be lent, resold, hired out or otherwise circulated, without the publisher's prior consent, in any form of binding or cover other than that in which it is published.

www.ukiyoto.com

For Soumyajit Das. You will be my friend to the end.

Contents

Dignity's Resonance	1
Blood	3
The Last Town	7
Nolite Te Bastardes Carborundorum (Do Not Let The Bastards Grind You Down)	9
The Maiden's Boon	11
So Long, 'Fraid'	13
The Lethal Arsenal Of Rebellion	16
Crimson Chronicles Of Midnight Wings	18
A Flight To Remember	19
Expeditions Of My Consciousness	20
A Call From An Almost Forgotten Phone Number	22
The Day Before Leaving	24
After All These Years	26
An Old Photograph	27
The Dance Of Predation	28
About the Author	*30*

Dignity's Resonance

He found me to be undecorated,
Like a simple piece of white cotton cloth.
Without any imprints left behind,
By a past lover or two-
No baggage to carry on my behalf.
He gifted me moti ke jhumke,
In spite of knowing my apathy for gifts.
He thought he could purchase my love with it.
Never did he know, that
I had no piercings.
We had to fall apart.
Twenty years later,
I saw his sister one scorching afternoon;
On Manikarnika Ghat,
Breaking her bangles and crumbling in grief
Like a wilting flower.
I took her to my home,
Gave her a glass of water,
And the box which contained the jhumkas
Her brother had burdened me with.
I told her to not let anyone strip her off anything-
Be it a vermillion saree, or her dignity.
She looked at me and smiled,
Then passed the hook
Through the lobe of her ear.

The jhumkas may have been expensive; but a woman who knows her worth, is priceless.

Blood

My back hurts like a mother on labour;
And even though I am young, I am old-
And my world mostly revolves around me
Except the moments when it doesn't
Like when my mother and I
Go to a shop to buy groceries
And she yells at the workers
Like nobody should ever be yelled at.
At moments like those
The pain from my back travels round my body again and again and again
And finally lands on my chest with a thump.
At times like those
I am grateful that she bore me in her belly
And gave me the most precious gift one could ever give someone:
Time, labour, respect, and love.
But that was a long time ago.
The lack of warmth in her is haunting,
Her lack of empathy, even more so.
The world wages a war on mankind everyday, all the time
There is no need to make them suffer some more.
There is no kindness. even lesser honesty.
Strange how life hardens magma into rock
Just like a young woman
Who used to sing lullabies to her daughter

While rocking her to sleep, on misty blue evenings

Has forgotten what melodies are

And how they harbour magic.

Maybe that's what time usually does to people,

But I believe that there are people who do not get coarsened with time and its cruelty.

That that cannot be the truth, there has to be another way.

She loses love like I lose my wallet on my drunken nights of misery.

All she has been reduced to, is loss.

Loss of innocence, of happiness, of value, of selflessness, of sentiment, of depth, of life.

Romance is not the only thing which turns sour.

When there is no respect between two people, or even things,

They inevitably fall apart.

But mothers and daughters don't break up, they remain under the same roof built of painful words as sharp as a katana which always strikes from the back,

Create unnecessary mayhem which rattles the dishes in the kitchen and scares my dogs, tormented nights with turbulent thoughts,

And regret, lots of it.

Especially not single mothers who have raised their daughters all alone,

They are dangerous and manipulative and powerful,

Because they have been fighting with the world for a long, long time

All alone,

And they have won.

So even though I am old enough to know what I want to be, I don't.

All I know,

Is who I do not want to be like.

Samara

My mother loves me,

Pardoning me for my share of negativity.

After all, she could have done so much, if I was a still born.

She loved the fork in her road,

But bitterness has eventually seeped in through its tines.

It is a weird kind of sadness, to have a mother and feel the lack of her at the same time

But there are more severe tragedies in the world.

I love her, not because daughters are supposed to love their mothers,

Or because she makes me,

Or because I owe her the love she has burdened me with,

But because I can.

Because I forgive her.

I forgive her for everything she has ever done to me,

I forgive her more for what she has become,

But what I forgive her the most is for becoming a mother before she was ready.

There still remains a plethora of wonderful things about her which I can scream at the top of my lungs from the top of the tallest building of the earth.

My love for her remembers that she too must have been like me once,

Naive and sad, yet still hopeful.

Only if she had chosen a different life,

Things could have been

Different.

But different is not how it is

And time is running away

So even though my world mostly revolves around me

I sometimes spare a moment to thank my grief for the sheer epicness of it,

And myself, for having the strength to not let it consume me. (well, mostly.)

Even though there is so much suffering and agony all around,

The wounded do not always hurt other people.

My pain ends with me.

The Last Town

She took a wrong turn at an unfamiliar corner of the street
Full of clockwork clowns who had
Forgotten that there was more to life than rush.
And the wind blew her black umbrella away.
Flying away from her at the speed of light,
Made her chase it, and forget what she had come for.
An unfinished business, like people's unfinished glass of liquor.

"Stupid wind,' thought the fly whose path had been altered
Unjustly, and landed on the top of the dirty nose
Of a reckless boy, not so reckless anymore.
He stopped to pick up a shining shilling
And rushed to buy an apple to learn
That it was not enough for even a bus ride home.
Too much disappointment, inside five dirty little, clenched fingers.

A lavish English breakfast, an apple, and two glasses of Chambertin later,
A scarlet woman turned white in her mind's eye.
The courtesan, wearing only a crimson-laced brassiere,
Travelled to her rebellious youth, when the last thing
She learned was, rainbows were painted of insanity
And with one strike of cold reality, was back to tend to perversion.
The expense of life, obedience over grief.

In a messed-up bed, the last cigarette burnt out as fast as the rise and fall

Of a chest that had been speeding to reach a climax,

Or to chase a flying black umbrella in an unspoken town of

Miserable and dirty little boys, and lost flies

Trying to find their way back to an English breakfast

Lying at the corner-table of a messed-up room, forgotten.

The walls wept with the woe of the hearts, and the room reeked of death.

Nolite Te Bastardes Carborundorum (Do Not Let The Bastards Grind You Down)

I am done waiting for everything to end
Once and for all.
They tried to strip me of my dignity,
But they are the ones who are naked.
What trophy should I put up on my wall to display,
When it comes to them?
Blood is on their hands,
The blood which seeps through my underwear
Into my clean, white, fresh bed sheets.
I would like to kill God, but I am too tired.
If this makes you uncomfortable,
My purpose is served
Because you never even blinked when
I was getting ripped apart and feasted on by vile creatures,
Or when night after night after night
I screamed in agony as I sawed my own body into two,
Separated my organs and hid them in dustbins
Or deep inside jars of salt-
Beyond the reach of crooks who like to pig out on them.
You kept on staring. Coldly. I wasted a lot of time
Trying to realize that this rotting corpse of mine
Smells of gunpowder, obscenity, and old balconies.
I am done throwing up on myself. I am done wasting my time,

Time which all the money in the world would not be able to buy.
These days I dip myself in glitter
And go out on the streets with my shotgun, named Asifa,
To kill people like you and them.
One is a filthy maggot, and the other keeps on staring. Coldly.
I guess blood is on my hands too,
But I sleep peacefully at night
And nobody can take that away from me anymore.
I no longer dream of jumping off my roof
Or chop unwanted parts off my body.
I wage wars instead-
Wars against rapist states
Which try to make me forget, but in vain,
That this body is all I have. All I have is me
And of course,
A rose,
A pen,
A shotgun,
And an army of wretched women like me.

The Maiden's Boon

In the ship with the broken anchor
Sailed a mighty pirate with utmost valour
Looting and plundering even in his sleep,
He had no fear of sinking ships.
Captain's hat, a crooked leg and two missing teeth;
Misunderstand not, his heart was covered in a sheath
Of evil stardust, which an evil witch had laden,
To rid of it, it was must to be touched by a maiden.
So guided by evil, he killed thousands of men
Innocence cried, and even the skies rained.
The seas trembled in fear, surrounded by gloom
For ripping the sheath, was the only way to his doom.
Disguised as a lad, a lassie one day
Joined his crew, so that she may
Escape on a voyage, no lass had ever dreamt of going on alone,
So that she could find her birth giver, her father unknown.
Downing crates of beer and reeking of cigarettes,
She camouflaged well among the rest of his mates.
Till three months later, on a night of full moon,
The Captain noticed blood stain on her trousers, a maiden's boon.
Dragged her to his cabin, and struck her hard
But as blood dripped from her lips, a bit flickered his guard.
Not once did she beg for mercy, as tortured as she might have been,
No such bravery the Captain ever had seen.
Stunned by matched valor, he presented her with a reward,

"On this journey, you may proceed forward;

But keep your secret hidden from my crew

Or else, they will have you for dinner, instead of chicken stew."

"Aye aye, Cap'n," answered the maiden and as she

Ran away to her cabin, the Captain felt a pang of glee

Which he could not explain, as he gasped for air,

As the evil sheath around his heart, had already begun to tear.

As days went on, he kept an eye on her

And his crew wondered, how he looked much younger!

In broad daylight, the maiden's and the Captain's eyes met

For a moment and flickered away the next, till she knocked on his cabin's door, one night late.

Legs, arms, tongues entwined, and hairs pulled right,

Uneven breaths, it was almost like a fight.

He showed her all his scars, some of which he got when he was young as a fawn,

Only to know that she would be leaving at dawn.

All the pain could not let him sleep

So all he did was hug her and weep.

And at dawn break, with a goodbye kiss and eyes full of tears, she was gone

And at last, the sheath was completely torn.

As they say, in the ship with the broken anchor

Sailed a mighty Captain with utmost valour.

Weeping for a love lost, even in his sleep,

He lay in torment, on a sunken ship.

So Long, 'Fraid'

They have found open water amongst the ice caps in the north pole.
I knew the world was ending,
But I did not realize that it would be so soon.
So much of my life has passed harbouring hatred
I never got to fall in love.
And now I'll have to bid farewell to people I am yet to meet-
That I would never get to.
How do I know when would be last time I am seeing someone?
T minus N hours remaining for the apocalypse.
I wonder where I have kept the book I was reading yesterday
It is hard to find things, people, memories in my clumsy, cluttered life
Perhaps it is for the best- there is not enough time.
How do I prepare myself to kiss my dogs and cats goodbye?
My tries to trap time are thwarted,
It is leaking out from a broken jar
I have to choose between a revolution or an apocalypse, fast;
Or it would be made for me.
I have not given birth to my masterpiece yet
I have spent most of my life locked up in a cage I built for myself
Sleeping comfortably, wrapped up in my blanket of hopelessness and misery.
Now that the world is ending,
I want to get a lot more mistakes to make,
A bit more air to intake.
They say that life begins at fifty-

When were they going to tell us about the lives that end before thirty?

My life is going to end before it has started

How do I make peace with it?

I do not want to be the misunderstood genius of this generation who tragically perishes young and famous

Because there would be nobody left to remember me.

I want to scream till my lungs hurt

Till I can scream no more.

Who do I blame for robbing me of my life?

I want to be more kind than I have ever been before.

Oblivion is so unbelievably near,

Why is nobody panicking yet?

There is not one moment left to spare.

Something tells me to wrap this up before it is time

The ants are scurrying to their nests down the vines.

Like two bulls charging at each other

With their heads bowed down and their horns pointed straight,

Spitting words like venom (our generational acquired trait)

We have spread poison like serpents.

What if I never get to make amends with my mother?

Will all be forgiven in the end?

All I see is a sonic beep and all I hear is mayhem.

I do not need gunpowder and gasoline anymore,

For the apocalypse will not be bigoted- it will devour us all.

I once read a story about a little girl from Jamaica, when I was little

Who was not afraid of the dark

And even though her mother tried to make her a'fraid' of the dark, in good faith,

Chasing ghosts and being chased by ghosts,

She never learnt.

You see, she did not know what a 'fraid' was,

And she surely never became one.

In the end, we will all be chased by ghosts

But it will be okay to be afraid.

There will never be enough 'what ifs' and 'buts' and 'yets'

The world is ending after all

There will be a surplus of ruminations and remorse and regrets

And I should probably wish for extreme growth or extreme decline in humanity on the charts of existence at this point

But I will not, for my wish will be rejected by the passiveness of mankind.

What would be more terrible than a billion evolved people walking into the end of time (as we know it) mindlessly,

Marching like martyrs

And working like clockwork clowns

Their keys wound up to fuck, marry, kill and repeat.

They have known about it all along

And I am the last one to receive the news-

The world is ending.

I never hoped for death to be kind.

If it is, I would shamelessly demand two last favours from it:

I hope I can dance to the end of the world;

And I hope there is music when the world ends.

The Lethal Arsenal Of Rebellion

We might buy arms from shady places,

But dissent, a seven lettered word, is the weapon of our choice.

We don't need to fill the barrels of our guns with gunpowder-

We prefer to use our pain as bullets,

And let it slice the ridiculous, shameful, unforgivable and unforgettable politics

Of who we call the King.

I use my weapon to kill the dictators who like to worship their Gods with one hand and feast on our flesh with the other.

They know not, that our agony gives us our power to rage.

They know nothing about the wrath of the people who have been deceived and wronged, every single day for the entirety of their lives.

They know not that we have nothing to offer to the world anymore, other than our resilience and might and vengeance. They have made us this way.

All they know is that a seven lettered word can be more powerful than gunpowder.

So, they try to crush our spine and leave us to rot in filthy cages.

They know not that we are like thunderstorms. We form when warm, moist air rises into cold air.

They know not how they heat us up; how we, like warm air, rise again and again and again, more powerful each time.

All the mothers and fathers and their children and their brothers and sisters: we rain down upon them, and when needed, we burn them to ashes.

Every tear they make us shed, will be taken care of.

Every fear they inject us with, will be showered upon them.

Every torment they have put us through, will be the death of them.
We will kill them with the seven lettered weapon of our choice.
We are going to wage wars and emerge victorious.
And history will bear witness to it all.

Crimson Chronicles Of Midnight Wings

Two birds flied
In the middle of the night
Beyond the blood and soot of the town
One flew left
And the other flew right,
And another one was shot down.
The third one was
The first to make a fuss
Hence the first one to be shot down
And then they followed
After the other two
And the seed to their graves were sown.
We never knew
That the birds who flew,
In their own blood they had to drown;
All we knew
Was the hope, that they made us hold on to
And with that, we set fire to the crown.

A Flight To Remember

Mamo *(noun)*: Mamo or woo-woo is a common name for two species of extinct birds. Together with the extant 'I'iwi they make up the genus Drepanis. These nectarivorous finches were endemic to Hawaii but are now extinct.

A Mamo wanted to fly
On a chilly, windless, winter night
For one last time,
Over the hills, within her reach,
Before the sun rose upon the horizon
And took her wings away.
She left her footprints behind
On the hill borne snow,
Something for her kids
To remember her by.
For a Mamo,
Winters on the hills are almost invisible, unseen,
Just like death.

29$ for a crayon set.
299$ for a Mamo wig.

Expeditions Of My Consciousness

My head is a canopy of never-ending convictions.
It is a sickle and a hammer,
Sometimes a pen, and at other times, a sword.
It is bitter black, sour green, salty cream and tangy red-
Or candy rainbow.
It is shapeless as slime, ever transcending like water
A misfit, an oddball, the black sheep.
It is sorrow, torment and rage
It is humiliation hidden in its cocoon of self-loathing.
It is a blurred mess of faces fighting to be remembered
It is a swift push of forgetfulness and loss of inhibitions.
It is as rigid, yet fragile as a straight white man's ego
Filthy, shameful, disgusting.
It is a cloud of hope,
That can bring down the rain of relief.
It is the smell of the raw skin
Of my newborn baby sister.
It is the warmth of my cat purring against me.
It is diseased with alcohol and loneliness.
Yet sometimes,
It shapeshifts into an eagle
And drifts far, far away beyond the lands,
Through a wormhole of loss and gain,
Into a spotless land of petals and glee
Never to return.

Sometimes, it just stays in its place
Staring at the ceiling judging it,
For judging itself.
It just depends on the day.

A Call From An Almost Forgotten Phone Number

I don't like when someone calls me

Calls demand your immediate attention, which is just too much expectation to meet

So I usually let it ring,

And sometimes I even sing along to my ringtone till my phone stops ringing.

I woke up today to sixteen missed calls-

All from a number I had almost forgotten that existed: my dad's.

Fourteen years of my life spent trying to get over all the grief he had caused us

All progression scooped up and put inside a jar, lid jammed shut

I was back to square one.

I contemplated calling him back, even made a list of pros and cons,

Added random things to the pros column to outweigh the cons.

Thought that it could be an emergency, or he might just be in trouble.

Forgot for a moment that my savior-complex was a result of his abandonment:

The story of my life, where he was the evilest creature of all.

I had waited and waited for a long time for this call, which never came

And when I was about to give up, it finally did.

It just took fourteen years, just a speck of dust compared to the bigger realm.

Fourteen years of a fatherless life,

Spent wondering what it would have been like to grow up with him

Fourteen years hanging on, without a closure.

Marriages fail, love expires, people get divorced, yet fathers who love their child make sure they know it.

I knew nothing apart from seeking comfort in older men who resembled my father

And then being tossed away in a bin after being their emotional dumping ground.

I drowned in a plethora of emotions before I learnt to swim.

I almost called my dad back, but then I did not.

The weight of him disappearing for another several years would be too much for me to carry.

I had made up and provided myself a closure within fourteen minutes.

My mother works fourteen hours a day so that I can live the life I want; she did not teach me to grow up and let a stranger yield so much power over me that I forget that I am a person of my own.

I remembered that I don't let anyone do that anymore.

My father would only call me because he needed something from us, I remembered him that much.

I added one more number to the block list.

To hell with fathers who abandon their children like I abandon plastic cups after I am done drinking my beer.

To hell with fathers who use their children as bargaining chips.

To hell with fathers who force their wives to be both a mother and a father to their kids.

To hell with fathers.

I am my mother's child.

The cons finally outweighed the pros.

I opened the lid of the jar, and let everything spill.

The Day Before Leaving

A skylark floats its tune at the edge of sunbeam
I never look back at my roots which have always shackled me
Shedding places like trees shed leaves, has become a part of me
And I wander on.
Nothing to carry but my spirit, which is free
Or maybe some memories which refuse to get rid of me
I wave goodbyes to airplanes that fly over my head
As I tread.
I lose myself in people and they get lost in me
Heartfelt goodbyes are things which I can never foresee
I never own people, so I can never be
The one to set them free.
I once had a life which was never meant to be
Waves of a lost life crash at the shores of my mind constantly
I do not have anyone to light up like a Christmas tree
When I return.
Leaving again and again is another way to let things be
I check my list and tie my shoes and wait for the sun to see
My face shimmering with hope, as I get ready for another journey ahead
Before I am dead.
I left my home at seventeen, a naïve girl full of glee
My spirit in my clenched fists, singing along with me
My mother told me to never look back, never to worry
She said, "What will be, will be."

Skylarks are my friends, and they tell me when it's time

To get up, pack up, and leave everything and everyone behind

No matter how much fun I have, no matter how much happiness I find

The day before I leave.

After All These Years

Her soul reeks of loneliness but it always perseveres
She gets her endurance from brewing storms and wildfires
She tries to catch her shadow, but it always disappears
She still clings on to a glint of hope, even after all these years.
The irony of life is when a clown sheds tears
I met her on a gloomy morning when she was all nerves and fears.
What a ridiculous game it is, played by the ultimate puppeteer
I asked her why she still held on, after all these years.
She told me that she liked to collect uncanny souvenirs
And on drunken nights of misery, she kisses strangers who like to smear
Her lipstick around her lips, and then at the infinite stars they stare
She said "That's why I never keep a count on lovers and years."
Even though our worlds collided, we belonged to different spheres
I danced through the jungle, running with wolves and sleeping with bears.
I kept my crown steady and I bore no heirs
For I know that I still dream of her, even after all these years.
My mother never liked me much; she still looks at me and sneers
I never liked her socks, or most things which come in pairs.
It is a false promise, there is nobody who shares
A moment of peace and silence, after all these years.
An eyelash suddenly fell on her cheek, of which she was unaware
She twirled her hair around her delicate fingers, and then tucked it behind her ears.
I looked at her just the way she looked at the musketeer
I still keep a picture of her in my wallet, even after all these years.

An Old Photograph

A friend of mine, once gave me a cheat code to time

As I carelessly kept on playing a game with it

And with each loss, one memory of mine

Would start blurring at the edges.

So, as shapes blended into colors,

I kept forgetting

Just like, with a flash and a push

Time kept freezing.

Nobody won.

Seven years later, I found myself hopelessly trying to remember the shape of my friend's face.

Death is more heavy a burden than time; and the weight of it, is always carried by the living.

I knew I had finally won the tug-of-war with time, when a dirty piece of old paper with grinning smiles

Decided to make its presence felt, chosen by my eyes.

A momentary relief that robbed me of a truth-

The truth to know that

There is always an end.

And that, we lose it and we lose to it.

Time never loses.

The Dance Of Predation

[The word- মাৎস্যন্যায় ; Pronunciation- Matsya-nyay ; Meaning: It is the law of fish in which the bigger fish preys the small fish and this law fits onto our society. In our society, the government resembles bigger fish and the public resembles a small fish. In this law, the state of anarchy rules the human society.]

As goes the folklore,
The shepherd boy had just two chores:
Protect the sheep from the wolves,
And get the fish from the fishermen on the shore.
Everyday he led the sheep
Into the grasslands not too deep
Collected the fish on his way back,
But before that, he would catch a little sleep.
One day when his eyes were closed
His herd of sheep was predisposed
The wolves preyed on more than half of the sheep
The sloth of the boy was exposed.
No matter how much he begged and pleaded,
The decision of his severance was seeded.
The shepherd boy went home weeping
That night, his food remained unheated.
The next morning they found his corpse
Hanging from the ceiling, with his face warped
His eyes as glossy as polished marbles,
His body was thrown into a pit unmarked.

This is how they all fall pray
To the higher powers at play
With their eyes closed, bleating like sheep
Forever surrendering to মাৎস্যন্যায়.
Time has come to open your eyes
And buy a jute rope for a price,
Then hang the seller with his own rope-
Bend the laws of nature to get out of fool's paradise.

About the Author

Samara is a dreamer, an explorer, and at times, an explosion of creativity. A poet at heart, she finds solace in giving birth to her creations, a form of cheating on life itself. Each poem she brings into existence is a dedicated offering to those who do not conform, to those who find themselves questioning their very existence. Through her verses, Samara endeavors to convey a message to these individuals — a reassurance that she sees them all, acknowledging their unique journeys and struggles.

www.ingramcontent.com/pod-product-compliance
Lightning Source LLC
LaVergne TN
LVHW041642070526
838199LV00053B/3522